THIS BOOK BELONGS TO:

Christine

© GGI

NEVER TRUST
AN OGRE

by Grégoire Solotareff

GREENWILLOW BOOKS NEW YORK

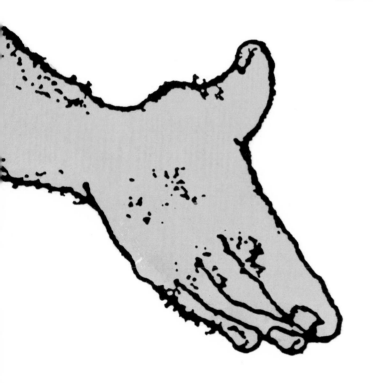

Once upon a time
there was an ogre.

He lived in a forest
filled with animals, but
he lived all by himself.
He had eaten his father.
He had eaten his mother.
He had even eaten his sister.
There was no one left to eat—
except the animals.

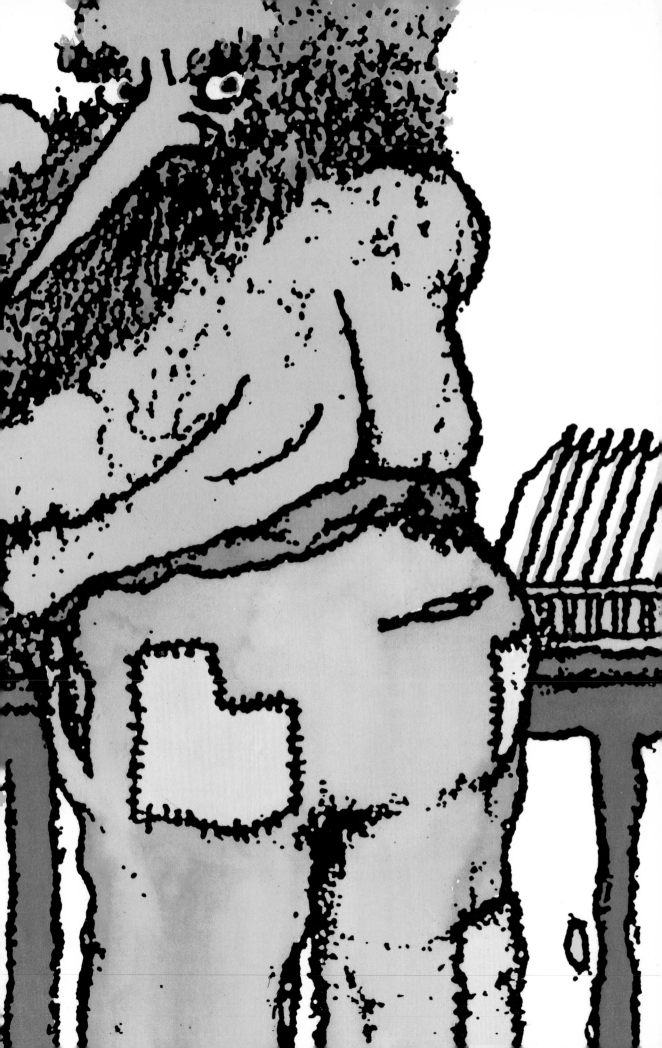

So that's what he ate.

The ogre soon grew tired of having to run
after the animals.
"This is ridiculous," he said.

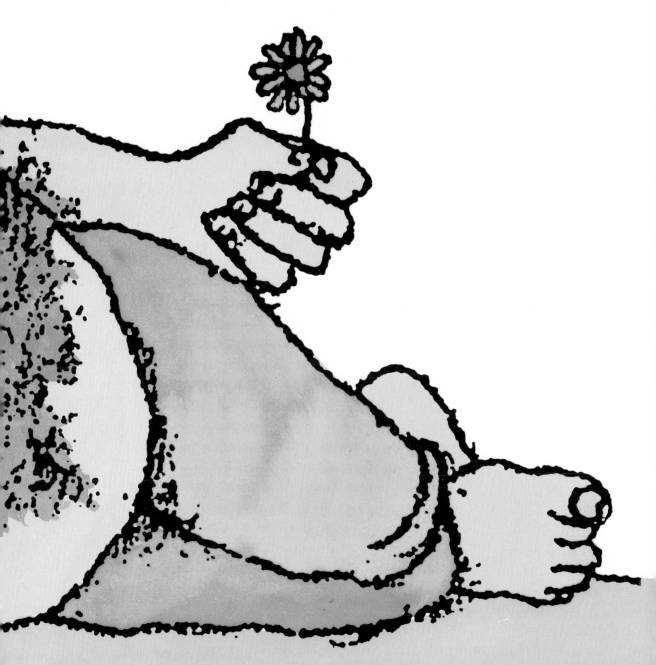

"I'm too fat for all this exercise.
I will make those animals come to me."
And he sharpened his knife.

The ogre practiced making friendly faces.

But it wasn't easy for him.

When he felt he was ready,
the ogre sat in front of his
house and waited for the
animals to pass by.
Whenever he saw one,
he would smile and wave.

The animals didn't know whether
or not to trust the ogre, so they
decided to test him.
They asked the rabbit to go to the
ogre's house.
"You are our fastest runner," said
the owl. "If the ogre is only pretending
to be nice, you will surely be able
to escape."
"I hope you're right," said the rabbit.

"My friend!" cried the ogre when he saw
the rabbit. "Won't you come in?"
The rabbit stayed outside.
"Don't be afraid," said the
ogre. "I'm not going to
eat you."
The ogre couldn't have
been kinder, and they
had a pleasant visit.

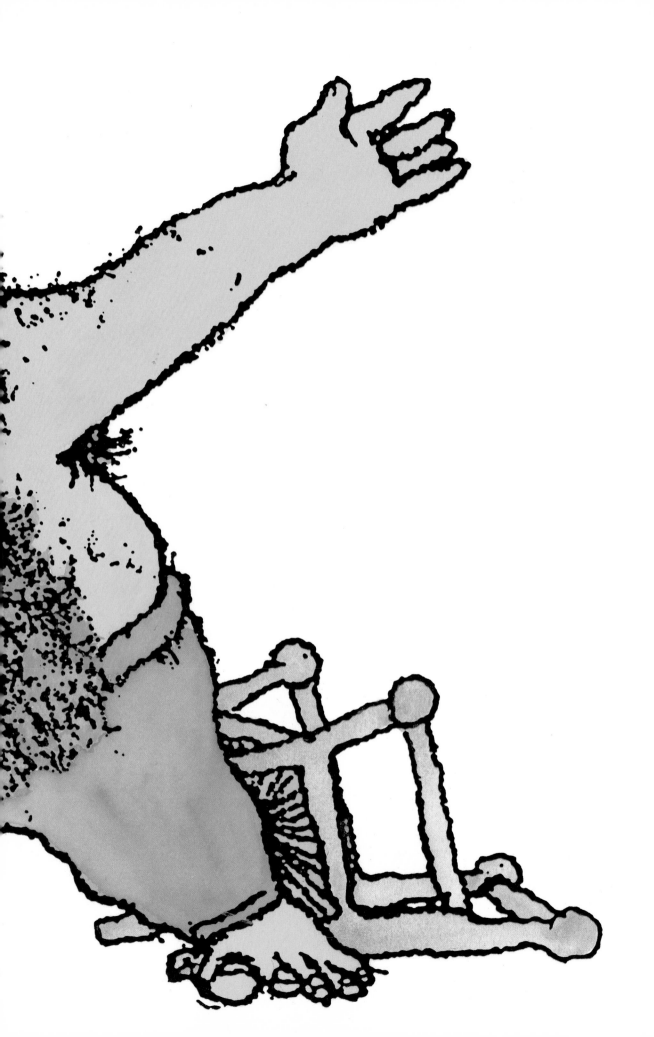

The rabbit ran back to the forest. "That ogre certainly has changed," he announced. "He wants to have us all for dinner."

"I'll bet he does," said the owl.

"A Friendship Dinner," said the rabbit. "He promised to give us all the vegetables in his garden."

"Sure," said the rat. "We'll eat his vegetables and then he'll eat us!"

"Let's give him a chance," said the old boar. "Think what a relief it would be if we didn't have to run away from him any more."

The animals decided to accept the ogre's invitation to the Friendship Dinner.

"You'll be sorry," said the rat.
"Don't come crying to me
when he cooks you all up in
one big casserole."

The animals arrived at the
ogre's house. The ogre was
waiting outside to greet them.

"Hello, everyone!" he said. "How well
you all look! How plump! How juicy!
Won't you come in?"

The ogre's table was piled high with delicious
vegetables. "Please help yourselves," he said.
"Where's your plate?" asked the rabbit.
"Oh, I'll be eating later," replied the ogre. "Hav
another carrot."

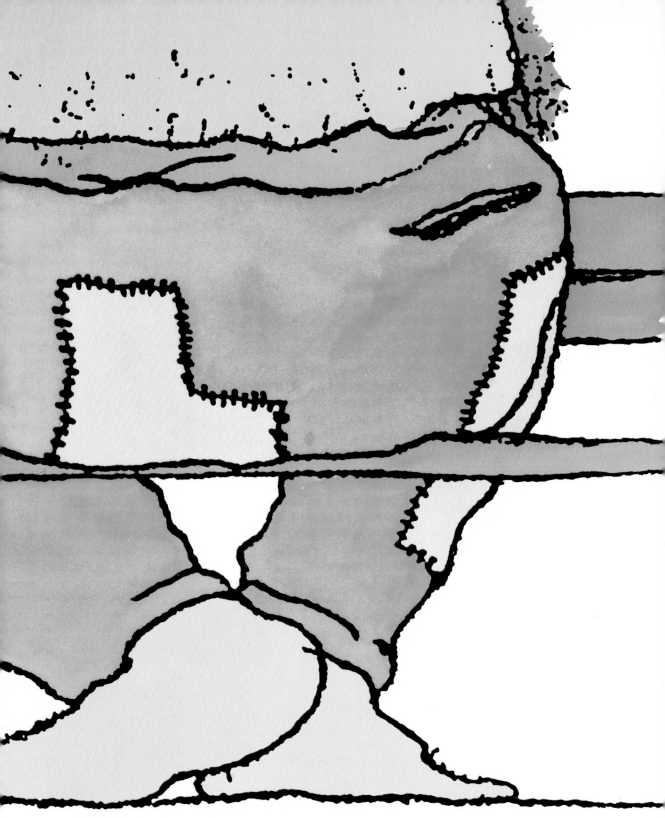

The frogs finished eating first. They
hopped off the table and onto the floor.
"What's that sticking out of the ogre's
pocket?" asked one.
"It's his *hunting* knife!" said the other.

"The ogre means to eat us after all!"
they shouted. "Let's get him!"
The animals jumped on the ogre.
The owl pulled his hair, the rabbit bit
him on the nose, and the frogs sent

all the plates crashing to the ground.
"You'll never fool us again," said the boar,
and he snapped the hunting knife in two.
Then the animals marched out the door.

"Those animals are smarter than I thought," said the ogre as he stared at his broken knife. His stomach growled. "I wonder if there are any vegetables left."

Back in the forest, the animals were celebrating.
"I told you not to trust that ogre," said the rat.

"We'll never trust him again!"
said the rabbits.
"Never, never!" shouted the others.
And they joined in a circle and
danced about with joy.

Library of Congress Cataloging-in-Publication Data
Solotareff, Grégoire.
[Monsieur l'Ogre est
un menteur. English]
Never trust an ogre /
by Grégoire Solotareff.
p.   cm.

Translation of:
Monsieur l'Ogre est un menteur.
Summary: A hungry ogre tries
to trick the forest animals
into coming over to his house
for dinner.
ISBN 0-688-07740-4.

ISBN 0-688-07741-2 (lib. bdg.)
[1. Monsters—Fiction.
2. Forest animals—Fiction.]
I. Title.
PZ7.S696Ne   1988
[E]—dc19
87-30239   CIP   AC